The Spirit Of
DIVERSITY

OBIORAH MOMIFE

LampstandBooks

THE SPIRIT OF DIVERSITY

ISBN: 978 – 978 – 993 – 754 – 7

Cover Concept by: Obiorah Momife
Concept Developer: Ezeobidi Chinonso

Printed by:
Asbot Graphics Limited.
No 22, Adifashe Street,
Ladi-lark, Bariga,
Lagos State, Nigeria.

Email: asbotgraphics@gmail.com

Author's Contact:
Tel: +2348077098851
Email: obimomife@yahoo.com

Publishers:
LampstandBooks

Oluomo Aderemi Jude Lawani...we met in a forum on Facebook, and you impacted my life so massively that I will never forget.

Rest in peace Sir!

Our ability to reach unity in diversity
will be the beauty and the test of our
civilization.
- **Mahatma Gandhi**

Diversity and Victory
A war is fought
in different battlefields
Every battle unique and different
What matters is that the war is won
for all
And all focused on the victory
Not the diversity of those in the
battlefields
With their different talents
Styles
Strategies
Mindset
All for the common good.

21.10.2021
Title: Chi Ndu Efogo

ACKNOWLEDGEMENTS

Felix Ekam, Cajetan Onu, Timothy Fakrogha, Obi Imemba, Kayode Akiode, Andrew Mark, Modestus Nwosu, Chinwendu Ememanka, Joy Ikeobi, Oge Nkazi, Ezinna Ogbuokiri, Henry Ikpa, Prosper Mbielu, Chinwe Owete, Hilda Dickson, Henry Ehuike, Imoh Efre, Chibuike Nwajiaku, Helen Ozeh, Chukwudi Amene, Obinna Akpaenyi, Ikechukwu Okereke, Olumide Akintoye, Tamunotonye Thom-Manuel, Awobadejo Olanrewaju, Emmanuel Nweye, Amenya Wokoma, Chì NDù ÉfóGò, Lucky Toyo, Patrick Somiari, Abayomi Salu et al... I am grateful for all your support. You are simply amazing!

Uzo Nwamara, Onyekachi Omenuko, Tomide Alo, Prof. Ebiere Ken-Maduako, thank you for helping to

prune the feathers of this anthology to
be able to fly.

The Poems

Yesterday, Today

There is no fear,
There are no tears.

The house slave that launders the master's
underwear,
Sponges the toilet yet
Believes he is master to the field slave.
He is the master slave that rations and starves
Other slaves that sweat in turn in the plantation.
He is the slave happy to be a slave
For he has access to feed everyday
Without sweating in the fields.

The innocent ones always hounded by the crooked
And the innocent suffers for his innocence
And naivety because crookedness is alien to him.

Some bats fly with birds,
They cruise at heights by nights
But day soon breaks, and the truth revealed, and
the skies are bare.
The dark caves soon become a sky for some.

I know this land.
I read of it and was told about it
I saw, witnessed some.
I swore the plot was an illusion
And the actors on stage clowns and comedians.
Seemed like a tragedy or tragicomedy.

I know him

He is a shadow.
I held him, yes, I held him
With these two hands.
Did these hands hold a shadow?
But how did I feel him?
A shadow!
An illusion!
Yet I was wide awake.

I know them not
They are strangers
Or are they not
Nightmarish guests
Or spiteful leeches
On the soul of truth?
Pack of hyenas loose
On a young gazelle
Ferocious sharks
On a lost sea lion
He is not a dingo
We are not baboons.

I think of yesterday's pain
I think about today's rain
I think about this acid stain
Ancient ignoble paths of gain.

They penned the tales
In their covens and groves
Painted saints, evil in these fables

They coloured evil as red roses,
Dirges become citations in this opera
They all thronged from their shadow
To walk in the dark with the twins
The thunder and the lightning
I am the sky, I am the earth
And I stand as the witness.

There is no single teardrop
For the fear is for innocence
And the victory of falsehood.

31 March 2015

Betwixt and Between

The mad man reclines in the dustbin
We take clownish roles rousing him
Who is bothered about this world

The drunk doze in their dirty gutters
Assets of ancestral maternal beliefs
Flood of spirits sink their troubles.

To the wise woman who bolted out
In answer to the call of impartiality
Lives a weird world of comparisons.

To the misty man who took to flight
Like his ancestors, ancient cavemen
Only two alternatives: run or rush.

They never change, posing to change
Becoming snakes standing straight
Softness bare, slippery traps masked
And walking sticks and electric poles
Precious time spent for choice;
The delicate seconds of denial
Not thinking before deciding,
Not planning before executing
Executing without reviewing:
Process, digress,

Regress, repress
Approve and decline
Synthesize
Analyze
Paralyze

Life depends on it
Time essence
Dying, living also
Obscurity
Fame
Popularity
Notoriety

How long... this lunacy?
How long... this nastiness?
And the madman reclines on his encircling dustbin
And the puerile lass lingers languidly on the brink
of lunacy.

05 June 2015

Pig Business

They wrestle with pigs in the mud
The man standing with a big rod
The one who has become a god
The one who is chewing the cud.

The clowns who file out in the sty.
The ones who in their closets cry.
The wise one walking by with a sigh.
The fool counting clouds in the sky.

The fight in the sludge gets dirtier
The bout increases, the mud gets whiter
Mediator in this scuffle seems an insider
Who dreams to dance drunk in the center.

They wrestle daily with the pig in the mud
The one who stands bearing the bulky rod
The one they all pour libations for like god
As they all lie on the grass chewing the cud.

15 August 2015

Stop Killing Yourself

Discover why you were birthed in that family,
Stop complaining and killing yourself.
Discover why you are planted in that marriage,
Stop complaining and killing yourself.
Discover why you are employed in that company,
Stop complaining and killing yourself.
Discover why you are planted in that church,
Stop complaining and killing yourself.
Discover why you are planted on the earth now,
Stop complaining and killing yourself.
Discover your purpose and vision for living,
Stop complaining and blaming everybody.
Once you discover your meaning for living,
You will begin to understand the reason for living:
The reason you are in that dysfunctional family,
The reason you are in that obscure backyard,
The reason for that frustrating abusive marriage,
The reason you are here now on this dying planet.
When you discover your purpose for life and living
Then you will stop complaining and killing yourself.
Then you will begin to live happily one day at a time
Because within your life is locked the future of
other lives.

09 January 2016

Diversity

He called me a 'tribalist'
Saying I have never supported
The President of my own country,
Not of another country, but my fatherland
He said, "Whether you like it or not the President
will stay his full term."
He also said, "You should go and hug a transformer
if you are pained and,
look for somewhere to hang and die."
He said, "You cannot do anything about it."
All because I pointed out a promise not fulfilled.
This is a wish of a brother-man for a fellow
countryman
Just for thinking and seeing differently.

I asked, "who is a 'tribalist' here?"
He also called me a racist.
He said, "You have not supported the pursuit of
corrupt people,
and their prosecution in the courts of our land."
I asked, "Persecution or prosecution?"
And, "Does the court need my help to find the
proof to convict
All who participated in stealing our
commonwealth?"
A wicked act perpetuated even way back from
1914.
I ask, "Do they arrest people and begin to seek
proof of

their culpability
Or do they ensure proof of criminality is clear
before arrests are made?"
Though they prosecute those that are against them
now
Those who stole from us are saints with them now.
Must I help your party fight when I know not the
enemy?
I wish I could be corrupt as you call me for not
joining your change
"You are sentimental, so unreasonable and very
illogical!" he said.

I asked who is a racist here.

He said, "You are a religious zealot."
"You are supporting the former President."
"You should pray, hope and support the present
President?"
I asked him, "I thought the elections were over
about 8 months ago?"
I asked him, "Did the past President not hand over
to the Present to lead all?"
I asked him again, "Why are they not focused on
the present but continue to pound on the near past
Just like they focused on the past President when
he was still President?"
I said, "Is it not zealotry to see wrong and claim it
will be right with time?"
Are zealots not nationalist, since they see the
nation not the people that lead her?

He is even a zealot… and calls this a saint because it
is him, and the old evil because it is not him
He is but a bigot, a die-hard, and attacks like a
fanatic fiendishly.

For being a tribalist
Perhaps, he was right
Yet we all are tribalistic at times
Yet, I know his tribalism is sinister.
For being a racist
I have no regrets.
For like all beings I got to support my race
Not against another race though.
For being a zealot
Stupid, but for only one reason, I am not their
Politician
Then, for a bigot
He is blind. He does not know he is now a bigot
Calling the evil he condemned good
Calling the promises they made unrealistic without
shame

I hate not the President, got no ability to hate him
He has the mandate of those who chose him
I will praise him when I see the good
Not the one these blind drummers scream

With tears from their hidden closets
Just won't call good evil to please
And won't call good evil to tease
I will call evil, evil
I will call good, good
So that those who do evil will refrain
And those that do good will sustain
And my mind its sanity maintain
So I won't become a hypocrite in my eyes.
It's your problem when you think and say I hate the president
Or that I love the past President as my Hero.
You also hate the past President with your propaganda
And you hate this present President with your hypocrisies
For true leaders know the need for honest counsels
And those who truly help them ride to glory
But I am better than you for I hate none
I had a choice, I made a choice
Just like you had a choice and made a choice
This is the principle of diversity
This is the spirit of tolerance.

29 February 2016

This Concurrent Carnage

There was a peace deal in Agatu.
They tendered their weapons
Then went to sleep and were attacked
By those who were to have tendered their revenge
Was there no peace deal for Agatu?
Was there no peace deal for everyone in this land
From Onitsha to Ogoni, to The North-East
To live together in peace as neighbours?

Now we have deaths everywhere;
Farmlands flowing with blood
Green lands littered with mangled bodies
Of those who trusted us to keep them
Of those who labour to feed us
From their sweat
From their blood
In the sun in their farmland

Was there really any peace accord?
Is there going to be any justice deal?
For the innocent voices hacked down
Deafening voices screaming,
Calling for justice,
Can't you hear them?
Can't you feel the gathering clouds swelling?
Threatening to pour hot magma like a boiling
volcano
On all of us as we stand like statues staring into
space?

04 March 2016

To all the innocent... slain in the new Nigerian theater of bloodbath.

The Science of Blaming

The blame game continues
O Nigerians
I blame you
You blame me
We blame them
They blame us
They blame our ancestors
Our ancestors blame their ancestors

Na you thief am!
No, na you chop am!
No, na dem thief am
Yes, yes na una chop am
Thief!
Ole!
Barawo!
Onye oshi!

Oya slap am!
Kick am
Box am for face
Beat am with hunger
Nack am akpako
Turn dem all to mumu
Curse him mama and papa

Make una fight inside the dishallowed cell
Tear una agbada and sokoto like agberos
Oya blame the devil for causing the wrangling

The blame game continues into auxiliary gear
The suffering, killings and dying continue
And they keep blaming tomorrow's sun
For yesterday's thunderstorm
Even as they die with us they blame
Even as we pine away they are sane
And they go home to cry in their closets

05 April 2016

Shared Stupidity

You see
They set the music,
Go to sleep
And you all begin to dance the tainted music.

My hero
May be your villain,
My chief
May be your thief,
Your chief my thief
Your baron
May be my moron
My baron your moron
So you see
We are in the arena
Fighting
To defend
Morons,
Thieves,
Villains
In the name of
Heroes,
Chiefs
And barons.

Before the music comes to an end
They reappear to change the tune
As we continue the dance in delirium
In the discordant stupidity as jesters
As dying dogs programmed to bark
Chief
Hero
Baron
Thief
Villain
Moron
Laughing, fighting selves like people cursed.
Like cursed androids in a macabre dance.

05 April 2016

Seize the Day

For Tony Obanya.

Tony:
O' Poet
Again with your words
You break my silence;
With your revelation
You smear my heart
Something you also have
That I embrace and cherish
Values, Truth, Principles
Quintessential hallmarks of life.
Keep them my poet
They speak loud when we are long gone
For a short time, we are only here!
Carpe diem, good Poet.

Obiorah:
I am lost and need to be found by love,
The police of the soul
Conscience: dead or alive
Works with the values
The principles
And the truths of our existence
That we walk and work with.

I am lost and must be found

By the police of my soul;
Account for my conscience: dead or alive.
Like a film records all my works, and my walk
With values of life

The principles
And the truth of our existence
That we gloss over as we walk and work
And war in the battles of this life
I was lost but now I am found by the velvety hands of love.
I trust that the future opens a pearly gate for us.

05 April 2016

This Blaming People

Blaming does not build technology,
Blaming does not develop science
Blaming does not apprehend crime,
Blaming will never build bridges
Blaming will never feed the poor
Blaming only keep people stupid.
Blaming will never give us power
Build rail tracks and connect cities.
Blaming will never make airplanes
Build skyscrapers and submarines
Will not teach values and principles
Will not retrain our dying cultures
Blaming does not resolve problems
Blaming does not make any nation
Blaming does not connect any people.

It is your responsibility you fool!
Shut up! it's your gaffe you idiot.
And they all age and fade away
And they fumble finding faults
In each other's polluted behind
Ignoring the power of the other
The loveliness of this diversity
They scratch the earth like fowls
Seeking worms to feed upon

When they should be like eagles
Swift like the horse on the coat.

When will this blaming stop?
When will we stop this brainless
Applause and this blame game?

20 April 2016

I Said Who?

Who is guilty?
Who is guiltless?

Who is a liar?
Who is honest?

Who is troubled?
Who is liberated?

Who is a thief?
Who is a chief?

Who is a moron?
Who is a baron?

Who is a sinner?
Who is a saint?

Who is tainted?
Who is righteous?

Who is corruption?
Who is fighting?

Who is deceptive?
Who is honest?

Who is irritable?
Who is peaceful?

Who is pretending?
Who is the clown?

Who wears a crown?
Who eats from the bin?

Who is our enemy?
Who is our friend?

Who is troubling us?
Who is healing us?

Who wears this mask?
Whose face is exposed?

I said who is guilty?
I said who is guiltless?

Who is this dark shadow?
Who will illuminate me?

21 April 2016

Celebrate Yourself to The World

Waiting for the world to celebrate you?

Let me tell you the truth
you may just be waiting endlessly,
and the frustration from it may be suicidal.

Begin now... Right NOW!
TODAY, to celebrate yourself to the world!
Celebration kills the bitterness that lurks
In the dark recesses of men's soul.

Celebrate YOU!
Buy yourself a special gift,
Take yourself out,
Buy yourself a bottle of wine,
Go to a big restaurant...
relish some expensive meals.
Go to the airport buy a return ticket
Travel even to nowhere
return with the experience...richer.
Enjoy your life, it's a gift from the father
Be happy for life the utmost gift!

Shut that nagging sorrow away today;
Those trying pain and disappointments
Weighing your sweet soul down always

Shut them far away from your life now
And never let them into your life again.

Stop wasting your time waiting
for this world to celebrate you
This world will only celebrate you
Only if they see something to glory
And celebrate themselves also...
start celebrating yourself now!

25 April 2016

Nothingness

Mold a skull with clay,
Furnish it with dried hay
Choose matters gray
Stuff in a brain today
Scoop the cranium again
Emptiness stays today.
Emptiness buds tomorrow
Nothing grows in this cranium
Why won't they cry like babies
Laughing in absurdity like clowns
Bowing and conceding their crown
And he joins the jesters in their tears
Rolling in the mud for this desecration.

They line up their dirty dais
Old fools filing after new fools
Fools that stand up for food
Fools that blame yesterday
To stay dumb in nothingness
Can't turn anything to loveliness
Only nothingness
From nothingness
Emptiness
From emptiness
Total nothingness

To blankness and blackness
And darkness stays in this skull of clay.

28 April 2016

As You Learn To Climb Up

In learning how to climb up
You should learn how to climb down too
To avoid a freefall, a terrible impact if you ever slip
So as not to hit the ground.

We all learn fast how to climb to the very top
None considers how to climb down without a fall
Without breaking our limbs if we ever miss our grip
So our spirit will stay sound.

How you climb trees differs from tree to tree
How to climb down must be learnt also from the
start
To avert a deadly descent as you ascend to the
highest top
Far from the ground anchorless.

When you learn how to climb to the top of that
tree
You must learn how to climb down from that same
height
Not to crash through the branches like a train that
cannot stop
Rushing without restraint into utter darkness.

05 May 2016

Until That Day

Until that day when every man will know their
limits
When we start to value the rights of our
neighbours
Yes, until that day when we shall all understand
And realize the reward of peaceful co-existence
We shall not just live to tolerate each other
But love and enjoy the gains in our diversity
Dream jointly in the array of our prosperity
Dwell in unity in our discovered diversity.

That day of the unity we seek will never come
Until we begin to value humanity as substance
Over and above material and corruptive fascination
Till we begin to know that unity is not tyranny
That harmony does not appear from injustice
That unity does not subjugate or marginalize.

Unity is not tying down a man to be in a dance
Unity is not heaping rocks on a dying donkey
To drive from a quarry up a sharp mountain;
Unity is not gagging someone like a mad mule
From expressing the heaviness of his soul

Unity is more than having one voice in a song

Playing happily on a stage while others listen
Unity is irreconcilable voices singing together
In one session forming satisfying sounding mix
A dissonance of diverse sounds forming harmony
Divergent colours forming a spectrum with a spin

Till that day we shall grope seeking light
Until that day we shall remain in this scary
rigmarole
Swimming uphill, downhill, in circles in these briny
waters
In broad day light while the world stays on her
tracks.

09 May 2016

Wishes and Horses

Wishes and horses
Paradox of pleasure;
Paradises without dreams
Daytimes and nightmares
Hopes and deceptions

Nigeria is not a nation
And we do not have national heroes.
We have ethnic warlords and local champions.
A thief in the East is a chief in the west
A thief in the South is a chief in the North
A moron in the South is a baron in the North
A baron in the West is a moron in the East.
You can juggle it anyhow, and it fits...
And, at the center
they grab for self,
for their families and their dogs
I wish we were a nation
A nation of people
A people who accept their diversity
With a wonderful vision
With a clear mission
Of a preferred destination.

I wish we had horses that gallop

And riders with a heart pure and true;
Minds set to conquer first their greedy souls
I wish we have men who tell yesterday as it is
Who see tomorrow as it will be.

14 May 2016

Before the Deal Is Done

Keep your mind on that friend
If you know any
If you have any
Many have many
Before any deal is done
Before they will be gone

Keep your eyes on that enemy
If you know any
If you have any
Many have many
Before that deal is done
Even with their still loud horn

Keep both eyes and mind fixed
On those superfluous smiles
Of that fake friendly friend
If you know any
If you have any
If any deal will be done
Even as they veil their form

Keep your eyes and mind fixed
On that careful cruel charade
Of that keen enemy

If you know any
If you have proven any
So, you won't cry when their deal is done
As they disappear in the middle of the storm.

Keep your mind and eyes open,
For associates and adversaries
Often do trade places
As in roles reversal
Without scruples
Before the day is spent
So, you won't die when their deal is done.

Keep your mind on that friend
Keep your eyes on that adversary
Keep your eyes open to observe
Keep your ears wide to hear
Keep your mind free to listen
Keep your eyes and mind fixed
To know when you become the deal done.

16 May 2016

The Men Here

The men here are like dogs
In the grip of this tyranny
Voices clamped can't bark
Afraid to wag their tails
Even to wade off fleas
Sucking their skin dead.
The men here are expired
Buried in this oppression
No dirge is to be sung for them
No requiem is prepared for them
No memorial is to be placed for them
The men here are as the wind, no sepulcher.

16 May 2016

Wailing

It is good to be a wailer
However, those that use the word
Are completely ignorant of the positivity of the
word
I am a certified, professional wailer,
I have been wailing even before most of them were
born.
I wailed for my mama's milk as a baby
Even as hostility of the Biafra war raged
I wailed when that bully and gang in St James'
Primary School
Benin City would always assail me.
I wail in prayers and moaning in my Spirit to God
I wail conscientiously for the growth and
development of life
I wail for justice and equity of the people of this
country
And wail when I see injustice and wickedness
everywhere
I wail for people to stop being historically selective
in their reasoning
I wail when I see educated people pulled by the
nose by stark illiterates
And as they accept all the gibberish thrown up
from their tribally,

Politically, ethnically, and religiously motivated
enclave, I wail.
I wail as people justify their error by believing that
one wails
Fights them for fighting sake and hates them for
hating sake
I wail as they fight and praise without content,
Without reason, without a conscience
Seems their conscience is dead!
I wail, and I am glad to be called a "wailer",
Wailing for democracy, for the rule of law,
For the liberty of free speech,
For all to consider the opinion of others in the
matter
And not be like fools running after fools without
any option.
I wail for this nation and her leader to begin to
understand the principles
Of diversity and the application of its principles
For the unity that has eluded us this long.
I wail because it is natural to speak against pain and
suffering.
It is abnormal to rejoice in pain
And praise pain givers as if it is remedy for insanity.
I hate to be like them, praise singers,
Hypocrites whose minds are perverted by the fiend
of fanaticism

The deception of sycophancy
The need to line their pocket
And stuff their bellies with political plunders.

Will there be a revolution here
Or just upheavals and shutdowns,
And storms that rock only tea cups?
There will be no protests for injustice
For justice is not defined in this land
We may have anarchy and destruction
And the thermal effect will reverberate
As far-off as our corrupted feet will flee
There will be no mutiny in this territory
They will cut many down like old trees
They will kill till every voice is drowned
That is what they always do and will do
Then new voices will spring up yet again
From embers of this thriving bitterness
They will burn their victims like old rags
Strongmen have shared us by our tribes
Even as we converse in diverse tongues
And hide in holes of mistrust and disunity
Hunger has destroyed the men on reserve
They have swapped their guts for porridge
Their tails hidden between their tired legs
For them and for their uninhabited heritage
We do not have men here anymore, just boys

Who think of themselves, their tribes and party
Do you now understand why I wail as I wail?

It is good to wail
To wail on real issues
I am happy to be a wailer
Wailers point where praise singers
Selectively become blind in daylight
Wailings becomes the poison of fools
Of cowards and imbeciles without brains
Who wail not in the streets but moan in their
closets
Those who suffer with the mass and smile like an
ass
Those who live like green snakes under green
grass.

25 May 2016

Same Thing in the Streets

Same thing
Everywhere
In the streets
In the districts
In the chambers
Even in the Rock

In all the valleys
In all our chambers
At every site and camp
Same thing everywhere
Same lawlessness
Same wildness
Same confusion
Even in the Rock

Sanity drops down like honey
Lawlessness flows down mutely
Wildness flows from up down slyly
Confusion flows downwards like rain
And all that is unpleasant brings pain

They are all mirrored boldly
From those who should lead
To those who ought to follow
And all are locked in groping

Pointing their fingers blaming
In this retrogressive labyrinth
Without any to steer the sheep
As this mad storm beats our ship

In this sea of sharks and suspicion

Even in the Rock
In the chambers
In the districts
Same thing in the streets
Same thing everywhere
Same thing in the day
Same thing in the night.

02 June, 2016

Experience

Barriers
Boundaries
Limitations
Restrictions
Pressure pressing
Sending out every juice from the mind
Hidden from the world
To lighten up the face
With a smile
For miles
And more miles
To break barriers
Boundaries
Limitations
Restrictions
Of our faces
Of our races
Of our diversity
For humanity
For harmony.

13 June 2016

Grounds of Victory

Falling is standing
Falling is crawling
Falling is walking
Falling is running
Falling is rising
Falling is living
Falling is falling;
Failing is failing.
Failing is falling-
Falling, rising, wisdom
Failing, running, great grace
Failing, falling finished
Romancing the fall
Finishing, falling, rising
Finishing, falling, running
Finishing, failing, rising, running
Rejecting the fall till the last moment
Till the very last breath
Till every fall becomes a story
Memorial left for all as history
A message of hope and glory
Told from the grounds of victory
The fall that brings the victory.

18 June 2016

Paths To Nowhere

Tell me how can this land prosper
As justice is taken from the oppressed?
How can this land grow
As teachers teach their pupils lies
And lead them into the maze of darkness and
hatred?
How can this land grow
When the past is unknown to the old
And the future becomes illusion to the young?
How can this people become one
When they are not and will never want to be one?
How can they dance and sing in harmony
when truth and honesty is alien to them?
Can a master and a slave be one?
Yet, they may be different and respect
their diversity for a common dream.
But there is no dream to dream,
to birth,
to build,
To nurture,
To celebrate,
Or have you seen a dream
Or a vision together preferred?

Only fear,
mistrust,
suspicion,
treachery,
blackmail live here.
Only its fangs and bloodletting I see
And human life like filth is without value.

Tell me who walks or runs in the dark
without a fall in this world of hurdles.

And this inglorious path
In their groves of deceit
This thunderous applause
From them who are bats
Blinded in their cold caves
To keep groping in day light
Tell me… will this people ever
See a common path together
On this their inglorious route to nowhere.

Yet they scream coldly to us to have hope!

19 June 2016

Blades of Hunger

This wickedness
Of men with power
In Africa
This wickedness
As in wickedness
Of men without hearts
Seems to be African.
This wickedness
Tortures their own.
Africans like them
With blades of hunger
with darts of starvation
With walls of separation

So, it was hailed with Biafra
That evil of starvation
The demon of kwashiorkor
That counted deaths
Of children of The East;
Of innocence
Of women raped
Of the old wiped out...
This is still being hailed by many
As if a curse meant for them alone,

This wanton wickedness
Left no lesson for Africa.

This evil stick with us Africans
Like dust of the Sahara in the harmattan
This wickedness
Seems to be the shadow of Africa
Like the shade of our skin
Or maybe the shade of our hearts.

21 July 2016
Inspiration: Ray Ugba Morphy

What I See

This is what I saw
This is what I see
This is what I'm seeing
I'm sure my sight is clear
My eyes uncorrupted
My mind not confused.

I stand for justice
Equity
Fair play
Rule of law
For upon these
A true future will emerge
Like a beautiful flower in spring
Leaving all these brambles behind.

I'm not fooled by these smokescreens
For a man that lie in the nighttime
Should not be called honest at daytime;
Prostitutes stoning prostitutes for prostitution
Pile up heated rocks for their own stoning.

This is what I saw
This is what I see
This is what I'm seeing

I am sure my sight is clear,
My eyes not corrupted
And my mind not confused...

What do you see?

28 July 2016

Perceptions

Perceptions
Opinions
Are freely the individual's!

What a man sees, he sees
What a man knows, he knows
What a man feels, he feels
What a man touches, he tells the story
As his heart will direct the plot

All remains with him, only in him
Prejudices must become acceptance
Ignorance must become knowledge
Unless his darkness remains with him
Even in the eyes that see the sunrise.
02 August 2016

Metamorphosis and Rottenness

This bleak
Dismal
Morbid
Reality
Of human existence
A glaring emptiness...

Then I heard one scream
"Do you know who I am?"
And I said, "Yes, I know who you are"
And he said, "Okay, who am I..."?
I said, "I bu nshi...!"
He said, "What did you say?"
I said, "I said you are shit... ordinary shit,
Just like I am,
Just like we all are!"

Like a beautiful flower
Under the spring's shower
He sprouts from the mucky mud
Unlike the butterfly ugly at nighttime
His ugliness trails his early loveliness

Think deeper you will see this emptiness
Look deeply you'll see the rot of this beautifulness
Boasting becomes toasting in a grill in a grim hand
And the sting is more lethal when the bloating
blooms

As his wings travel bare amongst spotted barbs of
life

04 August 2016

Wrecked Wings

The orphan is fed by his master
Just like the master's children
But we know when he eats
We know what he eats
We know where he sleeps
We know when he sleeps
We know when he wakes
We know how he wakes
We also know how he sleeps
We know the burden he bears
The scars that line his back, soul
The chains that invisibly fasten him
Within the boundaries of his shackles
And he sees his master's children play
Scurrying around with so much mirth
In the pastures that he slaves to shear
On the ground his sweat and blood flow
Above the skies his wrecked wings picture

No matter the power and strength of an eagle
A stormy weather prevents its accent to the skies
And do not ask me why the orphan turns out
better...

16 August 2016

Smitten Too

I have been smitten
Like a brimful fool
Brazenly beaten
Many times over
Even like a dirty wool
And left without a cover

Like a trifling tool
That never saw school
They made me drool
Like an insatiable bull
I have been smitten too

As you obey their rules
Could tear down their walls
But retribution restrains you too
I have been smitten many times

30 August 2016

Friend, Friendship and Sacrifice

Friend
Friendship
One you can sacrifice much for
One that can sacrifice much for you
One that will run the extra mile with you
One you can run in the night for
Not child's play.
Friendship is not a 100meter dash
It is marathon, a race that brings pain
And tries your endurance and stamina
Friendship is not what you take
Friendship is what you give.
Friendship
Friend
Are you a friend?
Do not seek friends when you are not friendly
Do not seek any to sacrifice for you when you are
greedy
Do not cry that you are hated
When you do not love...

Friend
Friendship
Not like the pond that stinks
Not like the lake so covetous
Or the Dead Sea that died for taking and not giving.
Friend
Friendship
Is the river, it flows freely

The stream, it waters distant lands
Travels through hills and mountains and valleys
Goes through transformation through dirt and grit
Becomes beautiful and dazzling as waterfalls
As fountains and seas and oceans
Friendship
Friends
Family
Life.

08 November 2016
Inspiration: Nosa Chinedu Iyamu

Walls of Hate and Self-Captivity

If you build walls of hatred around yourself
to chastise the world
you by chance build walls of separation
against self and the world

The world is yet to understand the power
of hate and propaganda
even in the souls of those who think they live
above misinformation

Only if the world will begin to value and learn
the language of love
then the world will begin to see our diversity
as the colours of love

To punish everyone, you build high walls of odium
around
you willfully build impregnable prison walls
against your own self

This world loves hate and hates love
yet pretends to long for love
and it seems that hate is winning
the battle, not love

As we begin to abuse one another
ignoring the ideals of friendship
Because of difficulties we face together,
and our diversity ignored

We need to redefine friendship
as we travel together in one vessel.

09 November 2016

Hand Lifters

For John Ugbe

Those that make others mount high
As the eagle to find a place in the sky
Deserve eternally to dwell at the top

Those that support others to smile,
To be blissful, to find an added mile
Deserve a path that will never stop

They place before you a stepladder
To climb to the height and not stutter
They will always be set apart nonstop.

23 December 2016

And They Kissed Before All

He said:
"You are the reason I believe in love"
She said:
"You are the reason I live to love"

Hmmmm,
How sweet,
How pleasant,
The songs of love sound
In the mouth of two lost love birds
He said:
"If it's only you, love gbakwaa oku!"
She said:
"Loving you is cuddling a hungry lion in a dark den"

Eheeen!
See how she is the reason he believes in love?
See how he is the reason she lives to love?

Have you seen the games we play?
Have you seen how we veil our lust with love
And run out screaming wolf at the first test?

And the innocent men and women in the city
Are out in the night with their hurricane lamps
Looking for love and lust to tell the difference.

Have you seen the shadows and the light?
Have you seen the scars and the treachery?

Have you seen them naked before a judge?
How friends and family are lost to the meaning
Of what they said when they kissed before all...

"You are the reason I believe in love!"
"You are the reason I live to love!"
03 January 2017

That Clock on Your Wall

That clock on your wall
That clock in your house
That clock in your office
That clock in your cell
Look at it now!
See as it moves mildly?
Hear as it ticks tactfully
On its concentric crossing?
Look as its second hand
At its minute hand
Even its hour hand
See how they move
See! they keep moving
They will keep running
As long as it is powered
They will not stop speeding
Into time, times of our existence
Time, the times of our destinies
Those moments we waste
Moments, we pursue shadow
Shadows, of nothingness
Nothingness, the fights and battles
Fighting senseless battles,
The fleeting flints of hate.
We throw into crowded parks
That clock on our walls
They will keep moving
No matter what happens
That clock on your wall

Cares not what you do
Whether you starve or you gobble
Whether you live or you pass away
Whether you labour or you stay lethargic
Even if you break that clock on your wall
Time will keep running ahead of us
As shadow we will stay behind
Or as light dart ahead to tomorrow
With that clock on your wall.

23 January 2017

Did The Blindfold Fall Off?

White goats in the day
Running around town freely
Black goats groping in the night
They are looking for stray goats
Goats that ate invisible yams
Fools all the time!

Dogs singing in the choir
Goats barking at the gate
Rats chauffeuring
Cockroach; *agbero*, smoking *gbanaa*

If you cannot mess
In the presence
Of your spouse
And Armageddon does not break out
You are in a bottomless mess.

The one tagged insane
To the one bearing a machete after him
"Until I look for my head then I will answer you!"

They are all expert liars
They believe their own lies
And walk home contented

Like one drunk with fresh *nkwu enu*

Again I say:
If the information mills sleep
The rumour mills will keep vigil.

So laughing is your hobby,
And you see those raiding mad people off the
streets
You continue to laugh like a hyena
I prophesy fresh chains on hand!
The more you shout "I am not mad o! I am not mad
o!"
The more injection go dey land your *yansh.*

If you hire monkeys to crack nuts for you,
You must learn to climb trees to take your nuts
Monkey *shakara* na because tree dey near tree.

Butterfly and bird things...
Negotiation and swapping
Chicken will want to fly like a bird
But will land and break its heavy legs
Butterfly will try to fly across fire
The traps and infernos betrayals built
Will tell the story of its broken wings

To the angry, hunting, hungry ants on the ground

25 January 2017
Agbero: Motor park tout
Gbanaa: Hard drugs
Nkwu Enu: Palm wine
Shakara: Showing off.
Yansh: Buttocks

Omnibus I: Defining Seasons of Our Times.

They call it coincidence
I call it calculated incident.
Teach them faith not fear
Show them God's love
Not the devil's devices
For Faith frees, fear freezes
Many "saints" barred their seed silently
Many "villains" bear their seed boldly.
Indeed, we are a very odd people.
It is easier to dupe who still believes
It's other people that have been duped and not
them.

Tied with some imagery lanyard
To some ancient shrub
In a grimy ancestral grove
Standing in the sun
Moping blindly
Like a giant
Can't see afar
Like a dinosaur
Extinct cerebellum
Extant fucktard
And around greenness
Of pleasantness...

Next time I tell you to look carefully
Into their past before you send them to drive your
future, you will.
Hypocrites!
Without a conscience they hurl stones
Even on their dead souls.
Many of us have done countless abortions
And in the eyes of the world are seen, as "saints".
Conversely, some of us had the boldness and
decency
To keep the children and we regard them as
"villains"
Is it not a vain and self-conceited world?
For some people, stealing is in their blood
And their bone marrow
They even steal what they do not need.
Like packing sand and putting it in their pocket.
And if no one sees them they will smile that benign
smile
That malignant smile of conquest over some
unseen forces
Some people's destiny on earth is to lie and lie and
lie.
They will lie till the day they will lie down to die.
Fela is dead.
Gani is dead.
If they were here many will disrespect them
But we honour only the dead.
Enjoy your evil and wickedness today.
Karma,
Nemesis,

Retributive justice shall possess tomorrow.
You will see!
How indefinite is this indefinite?
It was a rest, now a test and we wait indefinitely.
A quest now on their behest.
Zombieism
Loyalty without self-conscience.
The yoke of the leech and the dog gone to heaven.
Tralala tralala
One lives to lie.
One lies to live
One lies as hobby
Automated lying machine
And in this transformation there is no deliverance.

06 February 2017

Omnibus II: Same Old Narrative

Criticism points to where you may not be seeing,
Where it may be hurting others.
Ultimately it helps you if you are true.

Why are those that kill always afraid of death?
But there shall be no peace for the wicked.
Sleeping in the church makes none a Christian.
After all bats and crickets also sleep in the
Cathedral
They that kill with the machete can't stay calm
When one holds a machete by their shadow.
A simple mind does not understand
The complex network of corruption
You think you know the corrupt
You pursue those they pursue but those that
pursue may also be thieves
Corruption is a game.
You will never know all who drew the plot or share
the loot.
Corruption is like prostitution
Every prostitute has her reason for the job
Even "angels" meet them in dark places

The dog that barked when the chicken was being
stolen

Will relish its garnished bone thrown at it.
From the north to the south, from the west to the
east
Thieves are chiefs, and chiefs are thieves.
There are no national thieves.
Thieves sacked by one are employed by another.
Do not kill yourself for you know not who the real
thieves are
Or those who have become their bankers
Until a nation is born, we may not have national thieves or
chiefs
Or those pure enough to spot the thieves and chiefs clearly.

Tradition: Ask no question
Culture: Doing it the same way.
Africa: Why we are still in the dark.
Nigeria: Why we are so gullible?

God, please reveal the truth about this country
So, this acid rain of mendacity won't poison the
wise.
What kind of rejigging goes on in the brains of
some of us?
So pitiable logic is upside down like a baobab tree
So appalling that bigotry swells like goiter
How do you build a nation without historians,
economist, philosophers, psychologists, experts
and trusting politicians?

Some liars are so daft that before they become
perfect liars
They must have a good memory to always
remember the lies they lied in the past,
The lies they are lying today
The lies they will lie in future,
Who they lied lie to
When they lied the lie
Where they lied the lie,
How they lied the lie
And why they lied the lie

They call them stones for they cannot breathe
They come in different shapes
They never speak and you cannot hear them
You may not know if they can hear
They come in different colours
All beautiful in themselves
They speak to some people
Because they are all stones
They do not respond
Who will hear from all this noise anymore
The code encoded from those who can't
understand?
When you get enlisted in the rat race you become a
rat.

16 February 2017

Men As Toys

Men are not toys
Men are not toys for women
Men have not always been toys
In the hands of the women they love
Men will not always be toys for those that love
them

She who owns the toy
Knows how to treasure it
Or to tear it apart
In all generations men have been toys
In the hands of women; the ones they love
It was destined from time.
Resisting this is like the worthless resistance of a
fowl
To the brutal blade of the knife's
Attempt to slit its throat

Mr. Man, humble yourself, accept you are a toy
Madam accept the reality that being a toy is not
stupidity
But a prudent position taken to crown you the wise
one
For peace of mind of a wise man and a peaceful life

Why do we prefer mendacity to reality
Grabbing the cockpit from a toy that loves?
Plunging everyone into a deep dark mire
Why do we prefer ignorance to knowledge
Fighting over what will eventually drown all?
Why do we romance blindness?
We rejoice in darkness as one waits for the sun to
rise
Like one waits for his bride to be handed by his in-
laws?
Why do we dance to rhythms of lies from dark
groves
Squirming like earthworms in salt to godless
gyrations?

Men will always be toys for women
Men have always been toys
Men are toys for women
Men are toys
Tomorrow
Today...
Argue it
And be picked up from the wreck cold.

02 March 2017

Omnibus III: The Query

Androids, zombies, drones
Without a heart
Without a soul
Without conscience
Leading multitudes to El Dorado
Blindly leading their caged to their cages

It is written:
"They that diggeth a pit shall fall therein.
Sow the wind, reap the whirlwind.
Evil begets evil; good, good."

Gullibility is fostered:
Stupidity, ignorance, bigotry, tribalism,
Poverty, greed, selfishness, religion, colour, race
Only a wise man can act the fool.
A fool can't act the wise.
He may try but with one poke
His foolishness explodes in the market square.
Love is very wise, for if it hits you, you become a
fool.
Some are wise but end up foolish
Some are foolish but end up wise

More malicious to your well-being is that enemy rat
In your house than that unknown leopard in the
jungle.
She ate a wrap of *moin-moin*, threw the wrap away

She picked the wrap, ate the remnants with
thanksgiving

When the two streams of foolishness and wisdom
Flowing side by side come together,
Commonsense begins to ask questions.
Drones begin to romance the future from their self-
cells.
Those already locked down as generational tools
Recline with their megaphone screaming
How sweet it is to be branded foolish
To be certified angry town-criers.
They that are fools will dive back from the median
of reasoning
Into their glassy stream of delusion and foolishness
Flowing so beautifully in deception
Those desirous of knowledge and understanding
Will brace the currents of the river of wisdom
And struggle through the paths of loneliness
And discernment as anointed watchmen

Stop bailing water from other people's boat as
yours sink
You'll end up increasing the disaster around your
life.

That a man goes to a tree to scratch his back is not
that he is a goat

But because there is none to do it better than the
tree for him
The tree always does the task without complaint
They can't trust themselves why die as they won't
trust you.
They can't love themselves, yet you kill yourself for
their love.
Okwu agwu!

03 March 2017
Moin-moin: Nigerian delicacy made from black-eyed beans.
Okwu agwu: End of story. (Igbo)

When Stupidity Is Scarce

If stupidity becomes scarce
who will buy all the rotten eggs in the market,
who will believe that they have removed
what kills people in a motor car?
Who will believe bats eat cats
that eat up rats for breakfast?
Who will believe that children
come out from mother's mouth?

If stupidity becomes a dinosaur
who will believe that some people live to eat
Who will not believe that some people eat to die?
If stupidity becomes yesterday
Who will be the wise to run errands for fools?

If stupidity goes extinct
who will believe everything politicians say
after they fight in the market square
dance together in their children's wedding
reception
sit together as board directors upon the juice
That flows from our commonwealth

When stupidity becomes extinct
Freeborns become outcasts

And file out into the streets stripped
Raising bills printed by odd hands, sold to them
Dancing, praising shadows who steal from us
Hailing darkness who slays us to take our space
Task masters who killed our ancestors and lied to
us

08 March 2017

Sweet Rain

Rain!
Which rain?
What rain?
Rain from the sky?
Ceaselessly flowing
Breaking our banks
Forming waves of pain

Rain from our eyes
Torment and torture
Rain!
Black rain?
Acid rain?
Rain that falls as tears of joy?
Rain that comes as alert in the bank?
Rain that comes as love rediscovered
Found amid thistles?
Rain!
What rain?
Which rain?
Rain...please fall!
Fall for our vessels are empty
Dried from drought of fluid
Pour on these parched places
Waiting for your sweet nectar
To breathe life into to our arid souls...

Sweet rain, lovely rain
Come she is waiting

Come in a deluge, tender
Come to calm her longing
And when it rains, we will play
Even as some stray in the sweet rain.

09 March 2017

Omnibus IV: Mixed Multitude

Some run to love
Some flee from love.
Few live to love,
Others hate to love.

Love is life.
Love is death.
Love gives life.
Love brings death.

Once you learn to speak the truth,
You're ready to sit with your ancestors;
To share kola-nut and drink palm wine with them.

No matter how far into the sky the kite may fly,
It must stay connected to the one who holds the
line

You bend to peep into a man's anus?
You're only waiting for the world to dig through
yours.

No guarantee that a third wife will not taste
The lashings of the horsewhip as did the first two.

This scent called *stupidity* sells as hot cake.

And very costly too.
Have you bought yours?
No one even accepts they spray it.

The size of the mouth is not considered alone,
When swallowing but the size of the anus too.

Is it true that broken hearts never mend?
Broken hearts bereft of bitterness mend, even
better.

Bad men make good husbands.
Good men make bad husbands.
Bad women make good wives.
Good women make bad wives.

Conscience seared,
Minds marred,
Muddled for pocket
Souls sold out for victuals.
Who is next?

Crossroads: Place where lust and love, selfishness,
and selflessness,
Faith and fate, fear, and doubt meet.

Words are swords. They kill carelessly, wickedly.
So, keep yours in their sheath.

Free your mind and your soul from the crowd.

The cheek takes the slap; tears flow from the eyes;
The nose gives the mucus and the mouth cries.
This is division of labour.

Stop looking for witches flying *upandan with
brooms
When you are bitter with your neighbour's
progress.
Are you not the witch?

You prevent an orphan from sleeping in the house;
Even from sleeping outside in the cold.
Will you also prevent sleep from his eyes?

Conscience seared,
Minds marred,
Muddled for pocket
Souls sold out for victuals.
Who is next?

Love is like the sun.
Where you stand, it is what you do that determines
The value of light or the intensity of heat or both
you receive.
Check the hands of the iniquitous ones.

They bear very large boulders to hurl at the ones
accused.
Tune in to the music. It is melody in your soul.
And ignore the noise everywhere.
Pollution!
Avoid the insanity everywhere.

Without truth as foundation,
Without justice as pillars,
You'll never have peace as roof.

The love you show those who sow evil
Will not stop them from receiving their reward.

Stop looking for who hates who!
If you love, show it with or without words.

Your words are hateful, yet you talk of love and
peace.

It is not the enemy always that hates you.
It may be destiny's elevator?
Without a mad dog at your heels,
You never know your speed is as *PHEIDIPPIDES'

Education and wisdom must embrace each other
For sound logical and rational communication.

Do not mistake sincerity for stupidity nor stupidity
for sincerity.
When lies precede the truth always,
Truth becomes an alien:
An orphan that no one wants to embrace.

Once you learn to speak the truth,
You're ready to sit with your ancestors,
To share kola-nuts and drink palm wine with them.

This scent called *stupidity* sells as hot cake.
And very costly too.
Have you bought yours?
No one even accepts they spray it.

The size of the mouth is not considered alone
When swallowing, but the size of the anus also.

Is it true that broken hearts never mend?
Broken hearts devoid of bitterness mend.

Some run to love
Some flee from love.
Few live to love,
Others hate to love.

16 Marc, 2017
upandan is "up and down" Nigerian pidgin.

*PHEIDIPPIDES. *Legendary Athenian runner of marathon.*

Locus of Control

Where are you standing?
With a large crowd of hailers
With no mind of their own?
With a cold multitude
Of ndi n'eti udu ndi mmuo
(They that play the "udu" of the spirits)

Where are you standing?
In the sun of stupidity
In the grainy rain of foolery
In the hassled heat of a circus
In the torrent of this sandstorm
In this recession fresh miracles?

You can stand alone
To view the mass of grass
Rolling downhill crassly
In the dunghill of this yard
Into the furnace of serfdom
Songs for some new goatherds

You can stand before our face
You can rotate in the reverse
You can represent our rabid race

We can all take the dirty disgrace
Even as we all stand in the furnace.

21 March 2017

"Udu" (pottery-drum) Igbo musical Instrument made from clay.

Not Taken

The elites are taken
The police is taken
The military is taken
The Church is taken
The courts are taken
The unions are gagged
The senate is being taken
And we are all cheerleaders
Distracted, pursuing rats and bats…
Are you taken?

23 March 2017

Dances With The Wind

That time when you just dance with the wind
You spread your hands freely as one in ecstasy
You do not care about any spectators any more
You just boogie on the floor visible to you alone

That time when you just dance with the wind
Steps learnt from dance from a far-off land
And as you swivel, your perception swings
Interpreting rhythms, rhymes to only self

That time as you travel from the dance floor
Cautiously hang between limbo and liberty
To be certain you are on track from shame
So the spectators can still give their praise

Some may take to the dance of the spirits
Ignoring drumbeats but for that of their soul
Some will do this twosome on the sticky floor
They will never damage the feet of their love

The time when some with taps of their souls
Harnessed in symphony with drumbeats
Turned into bliss, into strange drummers
Of the soul to lead them to their epiphany

In this dance floor few will ever dance
At the time care no longer about spectators
You skip on the stage; two hearts, one step
As both dream away indifferently with the wind.

Seasons of Perplexity

This dying dance of shame
This curious silence for fame
This planned pursuit, a game
And they go on casting blame
Hot darts in harmattan so lame
To the lost souls without a name

Is this not a season of perplexity?

Fleeting festivity in the rain
Squirming orgies for grain
Freshly decorated by stain
Of blood sprouting for gain
From countless broken pane
Lining this littered land of mine

A deceased season of perplexity

Our heart a hollow grating gate
Wrapped in so uncommon hate
 Creepy odium growing so great
Hate that mutely mutilates faith
This hate belatedly appears late
No one seem to prevent this fate
Fate that has become so ornate
Hate that mere revulsions create
And this hate hunts like a hearth
State that smolders from the gate

What a serial season of perplexity
Their perplexity and our complexity.

19 April 2017

Omnibus V: Omnibus

You mix stupidity with intelligence and expect to give birth to excellence.

Vision without a clear mission becomes an illusion. May this dream not end up as a nightmare.

You cannot save the world by yourself, but you can save yourself from the world.

The human heart.
O how I wish they can see
This human heart...
To know the state of the heart

Despite all the noise, the best gift ever a man can have is a wife who is genuinely spiritual and fervently prayerful.

Once your bank dries up, their boats will never show up at your bank ever even if you do the "Mayday!", "Mayday!" chants.

Is it not clear to you now that perfection is not to be found amongst men?
Stop wasting your time!
On Laughter: All you need is your mouth. Try it now!
A smile,
A laugh,

A sweet laugh
Let the foe see you laugh. Your spirit will be lifted.

It seems here ignorance is bliss.
You can sleep in peace, wake up in peace, die in
peace and be buried in peace

Some men were sent to impregnate you; they're
not your husband.
Some women were sent to just bear your kids not
to be your wife.

You do not throw pebbles into calm pools and not
get ripples like dimples spread

Unless life is threatened ignore the call for divorce
from your "love".
It's tough, tortuous: In fact, very cold outside.
Church: many are rushing to sign the dotted lines.
Court: many are rushing to sign divorce papers.

On Marriage: If yours failed, stop being a witch
trying to make others fail.
Stop your lies and deception. God is watching you!
Wound from some tongues is deeper than some
sharp swords will construct.
He who denies a thirsty man water and a murderer
are Siamese twins.
You shared in my joy is not a must you must share
in my pain.
Get it! That will be your choice to make!

You see fire burning instead of looking for the fire extinguisher you are busy looking for who is responsible and who to blame.
It is easier to love a "submissive" wife than a cantankerous one.
Ashes from the old become manure for the new.

This patriotism slays reasoning,
This nationalism numbs logic.
What stands without sound logic and reasoning?
I am so angry right now that I feel like going outside in this sizzling sun totally bare to protest this infamy. Those who know the way run, they see light.
Those who do not grope, they see darkness!

Country:
Corrupt contraption
Circus clowns
Comely comedians
Compound cheats.

Waste no time cursing a man cursed, he is already cursed.
You can add to the man who is blessed...and be blessed.

Sometimes it is best to stand off the mirror so people can see themselves truly for who they are.

What is naked is naked even to the blind.

To the deaf the terrible noise of thunder is nothing.

Take it or love it! Real love gropes. In dark maze
love gropes. Real love's truly blind; those with
"open" eyes see not love.

Blackmail turns a wise woman or man into a fool, a
tool.
Once you detect the source, they are restored to
their default mode.

Patriotism can never be forced or legislated.

Patriotism is a conscious submission of self by a heart with a
proven level of love, trust, care and protection offered to it
first by a given country...or is expected to be received by a
preferred option to the present status quo.

Patriotism is a complex phenomenon and must not be dealt
with lightly

Your own child made a grievous mistake that
makes him foolish.
You disowned and disinherited your own blood;
does that not make you dumb and stupid?

Someone asked me if I can die for her, I said, No!
Why will I die for you when Jesus died for us?
My blood is not purer.

If you can't beat "dem" join "dem".
Nonsense!
So that they will be beating me always eh?

*Me sef go find people wey I fit beat to join too.
Enjoy!

27 April 2017

Spirit of Diversity

For Chinwe Owete & Hilda Dickson

Diversity
Unity
Prosperity
All over the city

Diversity
Unity
Our audacity
Our adaptability
Our prosperity

Diversity that stirs up sympathy
Diversity that upholds harmony
Diversity that binds communality
Diversity that plants prosperity

This diversity is a clarion call
This unity a place to stand tall
This diversity is so we won't fall
Prosperity for everyone in Total

Do you see the spirit of diversity?
Do you feel this spirit of totality?
Can you hear the echo of prosperity?

Embrace the pleasure of this beauty!
All over the metropolis
Proudly prowls prosperity
As we learn not to coerce unity
For the release of the spirit of diversity.

26 May 2017

Peace in Pieces

This peace is from the terror they give
The explosion and implosion of peace
Tranquility and deep drilling of this blade
Speedy sprouts from slit vexed snouts
This pursuit is to take us back to the medieval ages.
This is the time of wickedness
Times of uncertainty and bestiality
Times devoid of all civility
Times of darkened darkness
Adieu humanity if this evil is crowned!
Embrace you, reduce us with carnage.
What do you want with this "peace"
That you preach to us that spreads the city
With our blood and that of our offspring?

And the deafening silence from the walls
From the cities that this peace resonates
Bringing peace with pieces to our world
Please tell them, "take us not to yesterday!"
04 June 2017.

Smile From A Wheelchair

Soon as I walked into the auditorium
The glow on her fine face caught me
Ambience around her smothered me
Greeted her, she replied with a smile
Her voice sweet like fresh silky fur

I did not see anything like a wrinkle
Than the spirit of godly contentment
That ministered to my curious soul
Then I saw she sat on a wheelchair
She spotted my shock from my eyes
But her calm confident smile spoke
"This is my cross, I bear it cheerfully"
I spun in my soul, fell flat completely...

I interceded in my heart for a miracle
That she stand up from there and walk
But the steady smile on her regal face
Appear as if I needed that prayer more
To run with my two lively feet

Then her husband, a nice-looking man
Gave me the lesson for my entire life
He got up kissed her, rolled the chair
With their graduating son drove away
But I still see her face with that smile
I still feel that grace after miles away

16 July 2017

The Poet Writes

The poet writes
With short words
Longer than north pole's distance to the south
Words compact
Wider than the oceans.

For the heart of the poet
Feels the sweetness of nature's release...

And the poet's soul sees the dignified designs
For the heart to beat solemnly
And the poet's heart still beats
Like the heart of flesh and blood.

The poet's heart beats too
Like a train lost on another's track
It just keeps "tracking" and "training".

The poet's heart soon stops beating
But the ink does not stop flowing
Does not stop colouring our world
Does not stop seeking souls
Along poetry's forlorn noble tracks.

22 July 2017

Odious City

What is this reverberating din?

Hate, that odious spirit
Disgraces its hurtful host
Makes them think stupidly
Makes them speak foolishly

The more of the chicken the eagle despises
The more the eagle heads for the sun
And lets the old vulture carry the sin
The guiltiness of the hyenas
Let the goats bear the grief
And the baboons bark

What rancorous reverberating din!

And the baboons bark
Let the goats bear the grief
The guiltiness of the hyenas
Lets the old vulture carry the sin
The more the eagle heads for the sun
The more of the chicken the eagle despise

Makes them speak foolishly
Makes them think stupidly

Disgraces its hurtful host
Hate, that odious spirit

What a rancorous reverberating din!

Words from The Sanctuary

History records without colour.
Politicians shade the records for greed.
Intellectuals without morality
Confuse everything for everyone
They are meant to be our conscience.

Hate has no moral dimension.
Like money it gives life but (it) also kills
Like the blade in a surgeon's hand heals
Same blade in a murderer's hand kills
Hate can't be stopped with hate
Hate can be stopped by loving
Keeping those who question out in the cold
Hate is reaction just like love is expression
Hate locked up with time explodes or implodes
Hate is a regulator; it has no moral code
It frowns at kindness but laughs at cruelty.

To halt hate, you must eschew deception.
Hate bows only to love and love is truth.
Truth gives birth to justice and equity
In truth there is no fear or mistrust
Truth wipes away the pain of yesterday
Truth drowns every controlling spirit
And gives birth to liberty and prosperity.

When a child becomes a stranger at home
He seeks his paternity even from the streets.

03 September 2017

Hill of Lies

They lie
We cry
We sigh
Some die
Yet they still lie

Like a pie
Without a sigh
They boldly lie
Even as we die
Without goodbye
In this cloudy sky
No tears from their cry
In this old grimy pigsty

And they continue to lie
Like gods that will not die
Even as misery mounts high
They dwell in their hills of lie

06 September 2017

Foolery

You hide in your cubicle
and grin silently,
odiously mutating
like a chameleon
You say to yourself,
"Good for them, they
dare to touch the unforgiving one!"

When the leopard finishes eating the duikers
it will go for the moles in their holes
with peppered smoke
to choke them out...
Keep rejoicing as your neighbour falls
you will be the one to dig your grave.

14 September 2017

Python Dance

This Side:
The Dance:
Python dance in the South-East
Across the dark river for a voice
There's no dirge in the North-East
For this python to swing a dance
This dance theater is not a beast
To snake joyously in their trance

That Side:
The Requiem:
Your crime was calling for a future
Lost for years without direction
Entrapped in roving rigmarole
A sturdy voice of hope came
Though not seasoned, pure
Stirring everyone, all things
But it has to be cut down
For this our unity to flow
Sail On...

All Sides:
Crystal Ball
The circles continue to spin
All eyes, minds mesmerized

In this dance and the requiem
A fierce wind turns all the lights out
Silhouettes of mannequins prancing
Junketing and lying again tongue twisted.

18 September 2017

Peace is not Bound

Peace not war
Peace not cowardice
Peace not legislated
Peace, dignity respected
Let there be peace in this diversity
Let this peace drive truth and equity
On its very tender but hurtful wings
Let there be no master and no slave
For humankind must be kind to humans
Humanity must bring civility to their cities
For peace is not bound like a dove in a cage
But like a leopard in the field without restraint.

22 September 2017

In the Sand

That is what some of us are;
Hiding in dark cells of holiness
Tagging other people hypocrites
Hiding in cold covens of tribalism
Branding others they know not haters
Shielding odd and filthy faces of deceit
Without shame they call patriots wailers
Men who pray and wish we find true unity

Ostriches hiding their ugly faces in the sand
Hypocrites raising their anuses up to the sky

The earth will quake to expose their evil hearts
Souls that see black goats and call them white
Nose that smells fart but smiles it smells like rose.

01 October 2017

Tears That Can't Flow Uphill

And our happy new year chants
Soon faded with bloodshed
Then one girl returns home
And our games begin again
Blood sacrifices that keep us blind
Tears that can't flow uphill to them
Rain that must tear down the covens

Lacks the cerebral capacity
To comprehend the godly idea
Tagged the "spirit of diversity,
To know the differences of all.
Yet, like a crow you coldly caw
From post to post, outside the city
For the theoretical state of unity
That accepts that we are all one
And ignores that uniqueness
That makes us individuals
Special in our ways

Yet, silence greets this tired tunes
With bloody rhymes and rhythms
From this discordant orchestra
From ancestral hilly groves
That echo "not negotiable"

These blood were shed before
But they were the blood of slaves
Now the earth is tired of blood
Of guiltless blood of our babies
Of slaves who rejoice at slaves
Raped, killed by our complicity

Unity is not legislated
Unity is not nepotism
Unity is not hypocrisy
Unity is not the blind
Calling the lame for a dance
In a fast flowing river....

Blood sacrifices that keep us blind
Tears that can't flow uphill to them
Rain that must tear down the covens
And our happiness will return again
Once these blood dry up on the earth

They want unity
They want prosperity
They do not want diversity
Their unity is like the blind calling the lame
For a dance downhill in a fast flowing river.

05 January 2018

Unification

I hate violence
I hate noise
I hate wickedness
That is what we do here

I hate lies
Fabrications of evil
I hate deceptions
Pictures from the devil

I hate intellectuals
Who for mere victuals
Turn their seared souls
To feed on tokens of ritual

I hate politicians
Masters of magic
Doctors of miracles
Mutants and tricksters

I hate our foolish people
Lost in the labyrinth of lies
For tribe and religion will die
Smiling for their dosage of lies
I just hate being here
The hate of being different

Hate for not bowing to pray
Hate for now smiling in my pain

I hate this reserve mode
This pursuit to bring all in
I hate it that we are blind to see
That this is a prophesy unveiling

Maybe soon all this hate will fade
Fade into a million ripples of tears
Into a surging pool of flowing blood
Maybe then we all shall become one
Conjoined as slaves and slavedrivers

I hate violence
I hate empty noises
I hate wild wickedness
Is that not what we do here?

07 January 2018

Benue Basin Bloodbath

Wanted to write on the Benue killings,
The bitter burial but my pen stopped
For those hearts, those souls cut down
My ink ceased flowing like their blood
As a vexed vein for sacrificial offerings.
Held back tired tears for they died in vain
Can't stop my fear for the deed is not done.

As in the past the din will bring walls down
But soon will start to put up another so tall
This is why I can't start to wail and to moan
When the stranger that swallowed the child
Has his domicile in the womb of the mother

This is why I can't cry for these country folks
For I hear them say, "weep not for us no more"
Weep for yourself, for your dawning calamity
As long as you stay behind in this sinful city
As we must offer all for our bovine brothers

Light gives way for the night to envelop all
Darkness covers them all as tears to the eyes
When you are seeking rain from a deep valley
You need to know the duty of the sky beyond
And that rain from the sky also flings landslide
Yes, I held my lonely tears for they died in vain
We can't avert this fear, for this deed is not done
From their body language, their odour from afar
Dusts will rise as horses gallop again in the Benue

Like all other grassland and we prance like crickets
Marked for the oil they must surrender inside a pan

12 January 2018

Padded Pyramids

Padded Pyramids
Egyptian Pyramids
of ancient Pharaoh?
Nigerian scaffolds
of clean corruption?

So, they build scaffolds
pillars for rice pyramids

The winds have blown now
the anus of the fowls is red.
And we paid for woodworks
that increased our rice walls.
For the world a weird wonder
A signature of the new order?

15 January 2018

Outer Intersection

Power without conscience...

Cows and colonies
Rats and rattlesnakes
Goats and gorillas
Bats and battlefields.

Conscience without power...

Attitude is like smell;
Odious body language
Behaviour is like noise
Like bats, colour blind
As moles become deaf

Power without conscience

As the deluge draws nigh
Some hide in the shadows
Tints of tied, tired tongues
And some prance and dance

Naked without a conscience

Conscience without drapes on
As all mutated androids' mope
And the earth chokes for blood
Daily spilt upon her grasslands
Are they not lost at the crossroads
The inner crossings of dead consciences?

18 January 2018

Turncoats

Turncoats. They mutate like beasts

They surface with labels of religion
Seem guiltless but they have legion
Make pledges of ecstasy for our sins
Yet, they cuddle our sludge like pigs

They emerge in ugly veils of politics
Speaking, smiling to us like patriots
Like parrots with ancestral authority
Monkeys, defectors from out of city

Blackmail, not a mission friends go
Or hypocrisy a rest the brave flee to
Greed feeds this fire lines like drugs
They show at our gates as dying dogs

Then they resurface in attires of tribe
Old dreadful ravens made their scribe
Battles to spoil everyone as turncoats
With torn bloody pastoral soiled coats

And we embrace this sludge of tricks
We make pledges of ecstasy in deceits
We are blindfolded, they are innocent
They surface with a signal for a district

And we all assemble in this assemblage
Tired of throwing stones due to old age
But the scars from the patchworks stay
Over our wrinkled visage like baked hay

Turncoats, with their sharp blades drill
Of the jugular as mindless killers' claws
Turncoats, care not for anyone in the city
As they guzzle everything in their iniquity

These desperate deserters dark as coal
These turncoats, mutating without a soul.

30 January 2018

What I See

I see a sea of blood
Livid like a fiery flood
Run downhill as waterfalls
From their murky mountains

I see tired legs, a gory fate
Dive for liberty by the city gate
They scurry for the underbrush
The undertakers continue to push

I see limbs lost in this travesty
Fleeing helter-skelter for safety
But security ran off before sunrise
On the waiting wings of prejudice

I see hills, mounds of remains
Destinies ruined in dark groves
By this their confounded ferocity
Fueled by days of feudal absurdity

I see war only truth will subvert
Truth malevolence cannot prevent
I see dirty crows, vicious vultures
Hovering above every broken door

I see peace on sparrow's wings
I see hands raised to burn justice
I see the blameless, naive hounded,
All hacked down to stay astounded

I see that malignant bloody scorn
I see on his face that crooked grin
From the green fields in the jungles
I see dark standards raised on poles

I see burnt bridges from these cubicles
On the chambers of departed ancestors
I see a sea of blood and a dam of justice
Rise on the dunghill of defined armistice
But I see hurting hearts so heavy to heal.

08 February 2018

Swindling the Wind

They swindled the winds to ascend the peak
His malignant grin fiddles with many brains
They spin their mesh with worn-out silk
Leave their fools lost as butts in drains

This ravenous blade placed on the field
To cut down all walls to fresh fodder
In the mad muddle that can't shield
Their clear clowns in the border

As the goaded grip vises viciously
As the blood streams erratically
This silence becomes so deaf
The people's days so brief

Scaled below mere bovines
Tagged ordinary humanoids
People forgetting their brain
In cold flowing dappled drain

Leave their fools lost as butts in drains
They spin their mesh with worn-out silk
His malignant grin fiddles with many brains
They swindled the winds to ascend the peak

09 January 2018

Traded Places

Yes, he wanted.
Three times he tried,
he failed
Quit.
Wept
They gathered in their covens
They got scared,
Plotted, sent him out.
They needed him.
Thought they could make him a stooge.
They ignored history that they twisted.
Gave him power, forgot they move in a pack and
trusts none.
An agenda in an agenda
They know he has no business sense,
he knows
and his people know too.
So, his people surround him like a lamb,
paint the picture of a lion.
They are wolves,
won't let the lamb alone.
Those that led him to safety
are not lost
lost like a lamb in a lion's den.

They that watch the masquerade wear the mask
do not need to scream their names in the market.

17 February 2018

The First Day

Life is beautiful, but beauty is not the beauty of life
Neither ugliness, the ugliness of life
The beauty we feel stems from the ugliness we see
The ugliness we feel as we walk seeking existence
in life

The comfort we enjoy becomes comfort
If we had discomfort in our path
And our minds able to tell the difference
Laughter becomes laughter only if it comes from
the soul
And consciously acknowledging the pangs of pain
preceding

So is a rose not a rose if it comes without thorns
For its beauty comes from the ugliness of its thorns
Sometimes man is terrified
Sometimes he sports the clothe of courage
Both critical to appreciate the beauty and ugliness
of life

They say a wise crocodile stays near its own swamp
They say when a child begins to call everyone to a
fight
He has unseen beings as shield around him

I was afraid when I made this call
But now I have confidence because you came

As a crocodile, you've given me safety with a safe
swamp
As a child with adventurous teeth,
You have covered my large teeth from unnecessary
exposure.

I called you out today from your comfort
Not for shame, but for glory, our collective glory
Thank you for honouring my call.
Your calls in future shall be heard on the mountain
top
Kings and queen shall respond with their treasures
even from the vales.

The ugliness we feel as we walk seeking existence
in life
The beauty we feel stems from the ugliness we see
Neither ugliness, the ugliness of life
Life is beautiful, but beauty is not the beauty of life

29 February 2018

Powerless

A people caged can only kick
Show their power in chains
Inside their dark cold cage
A declawed lion enslaved

We are locked in a cage
Of atrocious tribalism,
Of noxious nepotism,
Of hideous hypocrisy,
Of slavish sycophancy
Of insidious idiocy

We see black,
We call it white
We see white,
We call it black
We see an inferno
Threatening to destroy all
We call it rain
And if we see rain
We call it sandstorm in the desert

We cry like orphans
In the hands of a cruel mistress
We smile like a goat getting sold
And as our hot tears of sorrow
Flow forming keen currents
We gaze blandly, pretending
Our hot painful tears are tears of joy

Accept it we are all caged
You are tied down in that filthy cell
Elevated treachery induced with idiocy
You are made powerless like a statue
With your broken baked hands
And tired twisted brains
You stand on a wobbly walking stick
You are locked in a cold cage of rage.

19 March 2018

Metamorphosis to Sainthood

They stole your commonwealth from you
You started running after them in the rain
As you run, pointing at them shouting, Ole!
They make a turn, running, pointing at you
Shouting loudest, Ole! Barawo! Onye Oshi!

And as they swap lanes, they become saints...

You all begin to bow, kneel, roll in the mud
Drones controlled from an ancestral grove
They make you praise them again as saints
With heads containing expired hired brains
As saints your commonwealth is so secured.

And as you mutate you become new slaves.

26 March 2018
Ole, Barawo, Onye Oshi: Thief (Yoruba, Hausa, Igbo languages)
respectively.

Dance Rearwards

When a child fails a class
we celebrate and promote him.
When a child passes a test
we fling him out to the silo,
into obscurity, into cold coma.

He failed abysmally
But failures praise failures
Failures lift failures up to cover
their shame, protect their failings
we are failures in all our ranks

Worst is that intellectuals
with dead consciences
Seal this perfidy of deception
Beat the drum of this macabre dance;
Dance that failures dance vigorously
completely nude, outside, finally insane
for their pockets to be lined, fattened
with crooked, corrupted victuals.

They failed abysmally
He failed profoundly
O what sin that opens this alley
for this consistent rigmarole
for this mirage in this horrid horizon
Breeding aged failing failures, extant dinosaurs
and the strong and vibrant are lost in the valley
their Hands raised hailing, bemused...

And he wants to dance to this music again

these macabre dance steps of perfidy
these drumbeats from dead covens
these inglorious dance of failures
these rearward runs into tomorrow
these telltales of accusing cockiness
O when the old recline to dream!

10 April 2018

Falling and Tumbling

You fall, you accuse the ground
That bears your weight without rent.
You fall, you accuse the old stream
Flowing faraway on its own course.
You fall, you blame the mountains
Battling with a passage southward.
You fall, you blame the sun in the sky
Rushing eastward to rest in the west.
You fumble in the dark maze of lust
You blame all those who found love
Even amid the spikes of rotten roses
You fall into desire daily dreamt of
You blame trees floored by the wind
You fall with mischief into yesterday
Blindfolded, lost, unfit to picture hope
You fall, you blame every banana peel
You and your troupe litter everywhere
You can't stand without hawks around
All the hyenas now howl with insanity
You keep falling, tumbling, and blaming.

16 May 2018

Car Owner

It's a Mercedes Benz
Aka ochie...
And the car owners
Are goats, reclining
Taking the last breeze
Destination unknown
In this cruel cruise
Goat, ewu mmee!

Out for recreation?
Chauffeur driven
Goats in a sedan
Intellectual goats
Goats on a mission
Goats in transmission
Goats without a vision
Goats and a conductor
In a dying Mercedes Benz
Goats, monkeys and Massas
Goats, goats, everywhere goats.

07 June 2018
Aka ochie: Igbo for Old model
Ewu mmee: Igbo for Goat's bleating

Different Molds

Some people are not meant to be married
They ought to be locked away as eunuchs;
Some folks are not supposed to be single
Reason they remain not taken, shadowy
Some people are not supposed to be rich
Their stinginess surpasses that of a child,
Some people are not supposed to be poor
In abject penury they remain very angelic
Some people are not meant to be educated
Their heads lack the ability to process logic
Some people are not meant to be illiterate
They saw not walls of a school yet are deep
Some people are not meant to be beautiful
The ugliness of their soul is unimaginable.
Some people are not supposed to be ugly
The fragrance of their presence is eternal
Some people are not meant to be in the city
They are meant to be in a bush as monkeys
Some people do not deserve to have power
For like hard drugs it turns them psychotic.
Some people do not deserve to be loved
They'll turn against you as hungry hyenas.

11 June 2018

Unban Our Codeine

But they banned codeine?

My chiefs are thieves
Your thieves are chiefs
My barons are morons
Your morons are barons.

Their subsidy is fraud
Our fraud is not subsidy
Stealing is not corruption
Corruption is not stealing
This change is not chains
And all our tongues loose
To sing the songs we love

Did they ban lizard poop?

This strain of nepotism
So strange to our ancestors
They discarded it for a knot
Knot that breeds nothingness
Nothingness their patriotism
Intellectuals playing politics
And redefining commonsense.

Did they lift the ban on codeine?

Have they legalized nonsense?
Did they trade sense for scents
Scents that smell like nwa nkpi
He says, "After all he's not a thief"
And others are now high chiefs.

Please unban our dear codeine!

20 June 2018
Nwa nkpi: He-goat in Igbo language.

March Southwards

They are baboons
They are local dogs
Their blood must flow
To redden the harvest…

They are hyenas
They are donkeys
Loved mooing cows
Silence for the slaughter

We are in zooland
The spotted one rules
Start the move seaward
Curb the reign of bloodbath

Monkeys grabbing bananas
These Lagos rats rush for fish
Cockroaches, this funeral dance
Mass burials amid times of peace.

27 June 2018

He Can't Find Sleep

He said, "Shut up! you are a slave, slaves don't
talk!"
Smiling, I looked him in the eyes and said,
"No, slaves talk, they need not keep silent
with chains on their hands, legs
and souls until the grave calls."
slapping me he screamed, "Keep quiet!"

I looked at him more fiercely.
He got scared
but remembered I was in chains
and he was free.
I hissed, "I speak, though I am silent.
I speak, without moving my lips.
I speak, without a sound that threatens you.
I speak in chains.
I will speak even without chains.
I will keep speaking to your wicked soul
until your cruel hands and mangled mind
Become useless to your existence".

Some slaves are in chains yet very free
Some slaves are very free but in chains
Some masters are free yet in chains.
Some masters are in chains and will never be free
Their bondage is the freedom they stole from me.
In their chains of change I sleep
but in their lies of freedom, they can't sleep.
For their bondage is my freedom they stole.

Atelophobia

She is too ugly
I can't walk with her in the day
She is too beautiful
Stronger men will take her from me
She is too tall
I will be unnoticed by her side
She is too skinny
What would I hold in my hands?
She is too short
She may give birth to dwarfs!
She is too fair
She will spend all my money on make-up(s)
She is too dark
How can I find her in the dark?
She is too educated
She will soon begin to speak big grammar for me
"You are suffering from psychosomatic
melancholia!"
She is an illiterate
I can't introduce her to my friends
Her mother is too tough
I do not want to become dumb like her father
She is not a Christian
She will become very materialistic
She is too "churchous"

Very soon it will be vigil with pastor everyday
Her waist is too small
She may not be able to have a baby easily
Her backside is too heavy
She will crush me one day if she is angry
He will end up marrying a blood-thirsty tiger...

He is too poor
I did not come to the world to suffer
He is too rich
I do not want who all the girls will be running after
He is too short
He will be like my houseboy
He is too tall
If I want to stand with a palm tree, I know what to do!
He is too gentle
I do not want a mummy's boy
He is too hard
I do not want to be a punching bag
His mother is still alive
I do not want a witch in my kitchen
He is too God-fearing
I do not want to marry a pastor
He does not regard God
One day he will use me and my children for money
He is too awkward

I can't be the one giving leadership
He is too authoritative
I don't want to be hearing, "You must submit I am
the head of this house!"
He snores every night
I am not marrying a bear in hibernation
She will end up marrying an ugly gorilla.

12 July 2018

Stars Falling from Our Skies

Stars falling from these hard skies
Tears dropping from our icy eyes
They stand starring at the still seas
Smiling with their deep scary scars

Stars falling from these hard skies
Freely on our deserted dirty streets
Their abode in the sky left in darkness
And the seas begin to rumble in distress

Stars falling from these hard skies
On the earth that subdues her increase
Stars stolen from our sky amid sinking tears
As the angry seas rush to screen their sparks

These stars will still fall from these skies
And their shine veiled with our wickedness
Blood that rises every day calling for justice
And the bowel of this vexed sea in angst threatens

We all see our stars fall from our skies
Lost in the amalgam of this barring wilderness

We dream tall dreams in dreamless dark nights
We wake up tumbling down in floods of mudslides

And none to hold our stars from falling from our
skies.

19 July 2018

I Kissed Her

I have kissed her
Many times, in the past
Though she knows not
Her silky, velvety lips
Restores my longing
She knows not that I kiss her
To give myself soul peace

I wonder if she knows
If she will give me a dirty slap
Or she will let me kiss her again
This time in flesh and blood
And with a very warm, lively hug-
Passionately

Well, I have her in my mind
To kiss,
To thrill me
To please me always
To restore my life.
I wish I could please her
Tease her too... passionately

But I can't tell you the lips
The beauty that I kissed
That made me see bliss
Now, I just kissed her again- passionately

We do not kiss and tell

As fools falling into pleasure
Telling the world of their treasure
That exist in their dreams-
A passionate dream

I won't tell of that lips
That brings me bliss
That puts my world in eclipse
Whenever I give her a kiss...
That kiss that brings me peace-
passionately

14 October 2018

Bubonic Plague

Yes, it ravages every blood cell
Renders their cognitive ability
incapable of perception,
attention,
reception,
or retention of commonsense

They become virulent in disposition
to everything that bows not
to the weird worship of this false god
even losing the common values
of respect for our humanity

Their sacrifices of lies
their rituals of bloodshed
the worship of their stomach
their vain, veiled, tiring tantrums
in this doctrine, a strain of dogma

Attack every opinion that threatens their god
they'll grip you like wild baboons
rip you open like a timid dog
and bathe the streets with your blood

Denigrate friends for their dissensions
Wise men in their fold are like nuts loose
they believe once you are not fighting
in their deluded battlefields
you are a coward
you are corrupt
what corrupt mind!

This bubonic plague.

20 October 2018

Chalice of Fear

You saw it as you drove down the autobahn
You thought it was an oasis for comfort
You stopped to drink, to quench your thirst
Behold it was an illusion, a misty mirage
Yet you camped there scooping "water"
With our ancient, cracked chalice
Drinking filth and misery
Dying in installments
Proud like a blind lion
Roaring, but in pain…
Only known to wisdom

And now you beckon on wayfarers lost
Seeking streams of succour to come
Drink from your desiccated hope
Of nothingness
Tantrums of the chicken
For the busy innocent pot
Victory of the mindless blade

And those who fight to become free
Are foes of those who endue captivity
Drinking from the chalice of their fear.

23 October 2018

The Artist

Until you tell me of your battles
In the stony seas of heart breaks.

Until you tell me of your struggles
in the shipwrecks of our existence.
Until you show me how your heart
got devastated, got renovated again,
Do not tell me anything about love.

Do not tell me that love is a feeling,
like a vessel tossed in the grim grip
of a merciless and tortuous tempest.

Love is not a feeling like the storm,
sailing eastward with the deep dawn,
roaring westward with sleepy sunsets.

Love is a choice, a promise to stand
like a rock stripped before the rain

Show me brushstrokes of the pain
on the hollow canvas of your soul.
Show me cold colours of shame as
memorials of your stony scars.

Show me the chalice that drowns
your midnights' tireless tears.
Show me your dripping pillows,
Sprayed with saline sweat,
before your old love frames
Loose on walls of delusion
that you know nothing about its
complex confusing contours…

Till then do not tell me about love.

16 November 2018

Impostors

It will take just one man
Just one man that knows the way
Like a tough tour guide
Through solitary twisting tracks
To save a city from revolting gloom.
Just one man is what it will take!
It will take just one man
A man who will give up his life
To save his people from disintegration.
One man that knows the land to take,
The preferred place to possess.
Only one man who is compassionate,
That knows how to hold the hands
Of those that will walk with him
To the land that they need to gain.

It will take a man who is sensitive
Who knows the people's heartbeats
To take them from depths of despair
To the pinnacle of their elation
To see the beauty of the horizon
To see the shooting sun climbing
To bring the rain to their basin
To make all bring in their sheaves
Into this superfluous storehouse.

It will take one man
To get all down to the valleys
To make them dig down to the earth
To make them begin to build bulwarks
To bring all scattered abroad together
In their diversity to blend in their tribes
To tear down every greed and folly

Yes, it will take one man
One man with a great mind
Colour blind to all the shades
Of human forms and idiocy
Truly transcendent, spiritual
Insensible to rituals of men
Lifeless to dogmas that keep men lively
In motion, as fast flying snails,
As the barber's swivel chair
To grow old, invalid in that salon.
We are not lost for we do not have impostors;
Impostors leading us into dark places
In this strange encircling burrows
We are lost for we have impostors
As little horns sprouting everywhere.

17 December 2018

Gall for Gullible

And the blind lightning
Scares night with light
Grunting gullible galls

Women without wantonness
Stripping in the streets,
Old men with no balls
Fleeing from their altars
Youths drugged down
Snaking away tomorrow

Credit to their credulity
Ignorance is knowledge
Stupidity is shrewdness
Prejudice is acceptance
Nepotism is nationalism
Loyalty their competence
Jesters in kits of thunder
Clapping hostile hands
Stamping bleeding feet
Feet of meridional fools
On buried barbed bushes

19 December 2018

Epiphany

For the equilibrium of love
you must have the balance
of stupidity and wisdom.
Stupidity to swallow that juice
of shame and pain.
Wisdom to stamp your feet
on the ground of integrity
and honour when the scale slants.
You can love
But do not be stupid
Enough not to be wise
To be playing in the mud like pigs
And not be barking like lapdogs

You can love but don't let
your stupidity sends you to death's throes
On the lap of flesh, the treadmill of blindness
where love lost exist not
And regret of lust breathes hard in pain.

So she asked, "Where do broken hearts mend"
I said, "Follow the paths of the old cross"
I see her rejoicing down the road
Though she walks alone her smile broad
And one mounting up another hill

With two sprouting stumps
To feel a fresh perspective
Seeking the soul of epiphany.

06 January 2019

Woman

For Lady Constance Ekeh

If you like attack me,
The next generation
is carried in the man,
birthed by the woman
nurtured to true greatness
by a strong spiritual woman.

Attacking me won't change
This divine spiritual order
Those who know knows
Man is lost without help
Until revealed you are lost
Revealed you see the light
You were sent to uphold
A standard raised uphill

He is still crude, unrefined
She, made in refined mode
How will she become crude
He can't become as refined.
On her knees she builds him
Helps him clear the cobwebs
Of his ugly nature for beauty
Of all the seed from his loins.

13 January 2019

Beautiful Gardens

Bleeding hearts
Flame of the forest
Queen of the night
Pleading hearts
And dying souls

Flowers from a lovely garden
Dewdrops from a fading soul
Droplets of blood on thorns

24 January 2019

Innocence

As a child I trod on prickles,
In innocence so pure.
Still prefer that innocence.

Picked up snakes,
Smiled at their tickled faces,
In innocence so fearless.

To shield a long "good" etched,
On my slate with chalk from rain,
Fled home to flex for Mum Alero.

Set out afore the cock crow
To that old gorge; Ikom, for my traps
And from a reptilian gift fled for fear.

One mission to Mama Nnukwu',
Alero's law, "Eat nothing on the way"
A bowl of water, a gargle, particles.

Her long wait, cyclic stopovers,
Clean hands raised to hail the rain,
Nimble feet splashing in the mud.

Innocence, dunes of emptiness
Sand dunes of barrenness
Sandstorms of hopefulness?

Still prefer that innocence,
To integrity we adorn in purple,
That steals our seed of somberness

Still prefer that innocence
Pure childhood, safe neighbourhood
And sweet tickles from mama's fingers

06 February 2019
Mama Nnukwu: Igbo word for grandmother.

Is He Not Just A Man

For Benjamin Nworah Momife & all fathers who sacrificed life.

The world lacks the skills to love a man
They say he should be strong like a horse.
The world lacks the skills to praise a father
He should lead, not plead like a weakling
Even if he breaks his back in the frontline
Or if he passes away with a broken heart

Heart shred into shards for lovelessness
Or in the passion of affection misjudged
Like a bull locked in a fight with a train
The man cannot stand without affection
The man is finished without true respect
We become dinosaurs as the man cries

The world lacks the skills to love a man
My mother would make me run errands
Back-to-back by calling me sweet names
She would call "Dandy" and I will smile
She would press me to the corner to drill
She loved me truly, my heart loved her.

The world lacks the skills to love a man
Fathers die with full loads on their souls
Fathers die with their tears not released
They are not meant to bleat like a sheep

But like a donkey just bray in their pain
The world deals illiberally with the man

I know many men perished in their agony
I see many walking the path of loneliness
Lazing as elephants to the place of death
Even in the company of many they love
The world hates the man for his strength
The power he lost control of its real use.

08 February 2019

Resting Place of the Foolish

The duty of the elders
is to tell the young the truth
so they don't get lost
in the wilderness groping.

Let the fools get lost
due to their stupidity
and their blood will be
upon their own heads.

The wise that will expire
due to the folly of the blind
will not stay lost in the wilderness
Or stay peacocking to a rock.

The fools will be chained
spirit, soul and body
in the arid sand dunes
of the deserts for eternity.

10 February 2019

Karma

Remember!
Remember the sizes
The shapes
The numbers
The colours of the pebbles
Those malicious stones,
And angry rocks

Remember,
The speed with which
You picked them
The rage with which
You hauled them
Hypocritically
Savagely
At them.

Remember how you continued
To lift them, throwing them blindly
Like a senseless preset device
At all those you brought down
Outside the city

They shall all be assembled,
Every one of them together.

They shall all be hurled at you,
At judgement
For justice
By invisible hands
As cathartic karma,
Malignant nemesis
For retributive justice.
And you can't escape them.

Remember, the very sizes
The very shapes
The very colours
Much more than you threw
Nothing more
Nothing less
They shall hit you at the point
Where your stones hit others
They will crack your skull
Tear your silky skin of evil
Leave gaping holes and bleeding pores
They shall sprout blood in torrents
On this earth that bears witness
And brings justice to all
Just like your stones polluted
The earth with the blood of the guiltless.

And you shall fall the same way

Your helpless victims fell.
I tell you, your pain
Will be more excruciating

But you have time now
To stop throwing stones
To stop this hypocrisy.
To stop telling barefaced lies
Spreading falsehood, you know not
Tearing families apart for your greed.

Nemesis is a worthy agent
It shoots and gets the bull's eye
Like karma calm like molten magma
Jump from the cliff of the mountain
You shall meet karma at its feet.

11 February 2019

Like Morning Ash

I dream of love always
But this Valentine's love
For me burns like wildfire

Heart beats like drunken drum
Drummer even drunker than I
I'm drunk with the wine of love.

My love and I by this fireplace
Will rekindle our true love again;
Love gone cold like morning ash.

13 February 2019

Escaped

Pharaoh's son sank
In the plague at sea
His gate-man's ward
Wandered westward
With the west wind
In the wild weird west

I will be here
To see the cricket
Get taller in a saucepan.
I will be here still
To see the earthworm
Wrestle with the hen
And a cock as referee
At sunup

It is good
We gain together.
The pain
We'll suffer together.
It's good we see
The clowns together
So, we'll see our laughter
Rise as sweet-smelling savour
Drown ourselves in tears
Not of pain but absurdity.
It is good we enjoy
This misery together;
Like a snail you can't flee

The fire that covers the field.
We shall endure the game
With our souls poured out
Without our consciousness
As we with our eyes open
Sow fire in our breast

I am an observer
I am free
I watch the dance
I am a heralder
I set the stage
The drummers
The dancers
The jugglers
Take their turns.
I am a messenger
I have no more role to play
I go back to the oracle
To hear of the celebrations
To guard against my captivity
And the release of my soul.

Friends
Fiends
Bigots
Here is your music

Dance it

Sweat it

Till the veins flow no more blood

Till the heart beats no more
To rhythms of cold-bloodedness

Pharaoh and all his men
In their power
In their chariots
Swam out of the red sea
With their swords whet with water
On a stone in the sea's cold chest.

26 February 2019

The Horizon

What is there now
Will it come to me?
Should I get to it?
Will it stand there as a tree
For me to hold and cuddle her
Or like the clouds float away
Like an angry stream downhill
To the voracious valley in the horizon.

14 March 2019

Time To Say Goodbye

For Laurent Blanquier.

We say welcome
When we meet at the gate
And as the day wakes
The moon mounts and time flies

Then we say goodbyes
Sometimes with a hug
Sometimes with sad shrug
Sometimes with laughter
Even as we chatter
Sometimes with grudges
Never wanting to let go
But with solemn pledges
We still say goodbye
To meet again
Just like the rain
Meets the earth
In their season
With a longing laughter
Like the sun climbing
To the sky again to shine

But we must wait
For the wind of life
To blow our paths again

We must pray Providence
To keep us from pain
So we will become stronger
Even as we say goodbyes now.

27 March 2019

Kamsisochukwu

Kamsisochukwu...
The last seal,
Chukwubuotam
A worthy shield
Not the least...
Chimeremeze
Charm so enigmatic
Enthroned to rule
Acts, and ways so thrilling
Love sturdy like eagle
Reflecting God's love.
May God steady your ride
To your place in the sky
From creation of the world
From the beginning of time
To our set walk into eternity
The Fathers' blessings are upon you!
Chukwubuotam
Chimeremeze.

16 April 2019

Till I Smell The Roses

This cold conundrum
This weird warren
This proud puzzle
This lazy labyrinth
Upon this crossroads
I must go the circles
Try the tough thorns
Smell the sweet roses.

I see the tape from here
I see the garlands
I see the laurels
I hear the cheers
I hear the scorns
I will keep moving
Till I smell the roses
Feel their tenderness
In these my hungry hands

03 May 2019

Drywells

Like nomadic birds fight to escape
From their waterless wells
Shafts dug with their life

A sudden realization of the hollowness
That we all at broad day light
Plucked the plumes off our wings
And like the whirlwind
Sowed corruption…

The drywells springs a fresh fountain

Helpless
Sightless
Caught in a maze
We take our turns
Running about the dark corridors
Of our darkened dry wells
Warming up blemished blood
Trying to recreate hope in hopelessness

Fountain flowing for foolishness?

We dance in the market square
Like *Agbogho mmuo and *Ijele

With our festooned masks
We dance our hearts out
In the crossroads of our dark wells
On the long stretch of our runways
Deafening praise greets our flightlessness

Fountains foolishly flowing in flightlessness

Featherless migrant birds fleeing
From their waterless wells
Shafts dug with our lives
Drywell left behind.

14 May 2019

*Agbogho Mmuo: Maiden Spirits (masks) adorned by men,
imitating, exaggerating characters (beauty and character) of
young girls, of the Igbo people.
Ijele: A big Masquerade of the Igbo people of Nigeria.

Her Grey Flag

This rain cloud was dark
I saw her rage from my yard
She coloured everything black
Spreading its fury over the sky

I hear thunder and lightening
Called for a peace conference
On the ancient Iroko burning
A fleeting armistice reached

Now, she seems not in a haste
Displaying her wet clout on us
Even everything seems so chaste
As her grey flag creeps over the sky.

21 May 2019

The Last Fall

I fall
I rise
I fall
I rise...

I learn to rise
If I fall
When I fall.

I learnt to crawl
To walk
To run...
Even flew for a season.

I have learnt to walk,
To grope in a maze
To run from a mad dog.
I have fallen many times
On slippery grounds
Where stronger men,
Where greater men fell
Where wiser men fell
By blocks that break
And peels that pull men down
With their faces on the dust...
I still fall sometimes
For fears that blinds
Like smoke in a forest fire
I still flee from yesterday's torment

The tears that roll for a broken limb
The scary scars of yesterday's fall.
I still rise for the cares of today
Blocks from hidden hands unseen
Faces masked without a smile…
I still crawl
I still walk
I still run
I still fall

I fall,
I rise,
I fall,
I rise.
I will keep rising
As I keep falling
Until I fall
The last fall
To rise the final time.

27 May 2019

Used, Abused

She pulled his clothes
She pulled her gown
They travelled the hills
Her dexterous hands as guide

And she cried:
Rape!
Rape!
Rape!
Neighbours gathered
They caught him
They tried him
They beat him.

He screamed:
I am innocent!
I am innocent!
I am innocent!
But she cried,
She moaned:

You raped me!
You raped me!
You raped me!
You will pay!

She pulled his clothes
She pulled her gown
They travelled the hills together
Her dexterous hands as guide
To his secluded cold cell.

01 June 2019

Tranquility

Once you discover yourself
You discover peace
The peace inside
You stop searching outside
You start looking inside
To make that heart inside
Better
Sweeter
Stronger
You stop comparing the outside unknown
To the inside known
You start loving yourself
You start being grateful
For every single moment you breathe
For every single day you see the sun
For every single day you wade through the
darkness
Of the night like in muddy streams

Once you discover yourself
You will begin to jettison the weight
That traps men's soul on earth
The garbage that traps the spirit at sea
Whilst searching for dew in the wilderness

When you discover yourself
You will begin to help others, lost in life's labyrinth
On this slippery, thorny realm of illusion
And disillusionment
To find a meaning for their battered life also

If you discover yourself,
You discover peace
For God is in you
For God is peace
For God is tranquility.

01 June 2019

The Face Of A Poet

The face of a poet can be ugly, forlorn
The face of a poet may be handsome, upbeat
The face of a poet may show fulfilment
The face of poet may be that of failure
The face of a poet may show contentment, joy
The face of a poet may show greed, anger
The face of a poet may show courage, loyalty
The face of a poet may reek of cowardice,
hypocrisy
The face of a poet may be bland, deceptive
The soul, heart of a poet is what the world needs
Not the face of a poet.

06 June 2019

Not In A Competition With You

Relax! I am not in competition with you.
Our paths crossed not to rub shoulders
Or to know who is richer or poorer.

I never in my life desire to be rich.
To be rich for me is to never
see a hungry soul and walk away
without putting a smile on that face.

Not to keep counting how much
I have saved, whose house is bigger
or whose car is faster.

I am not in a competition with you
for I know my hands one day will hold nothing,
my soul tied to nothing here in this realm
as I fly home to eternity.

08 July 2019

A Philosopher Is Born

For Wokoma Saate

This pain is not wasted
Pain that brings the world gain
Rain that brings the ground happiness
Grains that sprout greens to be a forest
Forest that the flame of the forest blooms.

This pain is not wasted
Pain that brings the smile from the soul
To say to God, I am grateful I still breathe
To say to mother earth, thank you for bearing me
To the wind, for bringing me sweet breeze for my
lungs
For my brain to still identify faces that smile with
me.

This pain will not be wasted
For though I can't run, I will teach many to run
Though I can't dance, I will sing music to men's soul
I will take them to the hills to see the beauty of life
I will take them to the valleys to see the ugliness of
life
I will make them see that joy yet flows from the
soul
Though the soul be burdened with pain.

My pain will not be wasted
This gain will be celebrated.
05 October 2019

Rose Bushes

You plant a lovely rose garden
And you despise rose flowers.
As the sweet roses bloom
You won't even smell a rose
You lock up all her wells
You will not visit her hills
You set up drones in her gates
To keep off birds and butterflies
To cross, not to cross her fading fluid.
Is this not wickedness?

You allow those ravishing red roses
Bloom and die of loneliness
Taunting trying triangles.
You let those precious purple petal
Beauty stranded in ugliness
Soul amok in the wilderness
Mind trapped in your thorny tracks
Unfit for your honeycomb.
Are you this wicked?

Sing you are not selfish!
Was she not tender in her nursery?
Now, you have suckled her with filth
To you she is now as fat of the earth
Unfit for your honey and the heat
Of your flea-infested fiefdom.
Your frail volleys and mud slings
The pleasure of your tyranny.

And you are not self-centered?

You are sly to let him dangle
Aimlessly about the city gates.
Know that many parade the city walls
Soon the East and the West will unite
Her rivulet will feed fat the hyenas
Roaming about your fabulous facades.

And you still plant beautiful rose gardens
And watch them grow into thorny bushes.

06 October 2019

Ships

Hips are traps
Luring men to trips
They may never return from.

Hips are trips
That trap men in the lips
Of pleasures unrestrained...

If like a vice a hip grips
It will pummel you on an anvil
And leave you battered like foil

They grope like sheep
On a hill looking for salt to sip
And every night for winds to grip

Hips trap men in ships
Luring men through trips
They may never return sane.

07 July 2020

Poison To Their Souls

They live in their hate
In their festooned cocoon
Breathe in their bitterness
Bile that will poison their souls

In their infantile,
puerile,
kindergarten reasoning
they think
because hatred and bitterness
drove their acidic criticisms
in the past
every dissenting voice
is motivated by hate
and bitterness.

What perfidy!
a critical issue that borders
on psychosomatic imbalance
of the cranial components
they carry in their coconuts

They live in their hate
In their festooned cocoons

Breathe in their biled bitterness
Bile that will poison their soul.

30 August 2020

Stones

I see beauty shades
shades of beauty
beauty of the spirit
spirit of our diversity
diversity in the city
city of complete joy
joy and sounds of bluebells
bluebells sprouting to deafness
deafness, stubbornness, silence
silence deadening beauty as stones
stones, shades of pebbles of sadness...

I still see beautiful shades of joyfulness
Joyfulness wrapped with trepidation....

28 May 2021

Igbo First

If you mourn your dead
and prevent me from mine
what shall I call you...?

If you mourn your dead
and I refuse to cowardly mourn mine
what will you call me?

To all those murdered
in those inglorious years
may your bleeding souls
keep vigil until peace is found
ancestors at heaven's gate
making intersessions for all...

If you mourn your dead
go on rampage about the city
and I refuse to cowardly mourn mine
what will you call me?
I am Igbo first....

30 May 2021

Dot

The dot
The beginning
The end of everything.
He prophesied the truth
But with an impure heart.

The dot
You don't mess with it
It is the center of everything
The fuel that runs the engine
Hate it, kill it, you'll still need it

The dot
May not be hot or cold
May not burn like wide fire
You can't put out it's steam
For it is from divinity, the source

I am a dot
The tiny jot in this rot
Bound by hate not to flow
Like ripples locked in a teaspoon
Of fearful feet of morbid indignation

I am the dot
David with five stones
That man at the pool waiting
The angels will soon stir the water
Then the four winds from the throne

Then the dots will become a testimony.

1233am, 12 May 2021

Reincarnation

And she lied there on the cradle, drained
After the surgical blades sweated all night
Staring at the ceilings that gave way easily
Into leaks of what would arise if she sleeps...

They came in their groups weeping, sobbing
I saw the one who never wanted me to live
She cried more than everyone in the family
Saw the ugly mask she wore while she wept

My business partner came with a false list
Claiming I owed him the coastline of Africa
Did not execute any deal in any waterways
See my cold list is sealed up in my old chest

Some came to see if it was true that I died
Not for any form of love in their dark heart
But to sweetly see all they owe me interred
Upon the deluge of their treacherous tears

Only those young ones with hearts tender
Like tendrils who needs my leading fingers
Did their tears stream freely with empathy?
Even as my drained tears stopped flowing...

Can a bird with clipped wings grace the sky?
Lying down here I see yesterday, tomorrow
Can a surrounded soul warn the weird wind?
Running around the city they can't see today

And she lied there on the cradle, drained
After the surgical blades sweated all night
Staring at the ceilings that gave way easily
Into leaks of what would arise if she sleeps...

21 June 2021

Pen Not Broken

My pen is not broken
But my ink runs out fast
And needs to be replaced
Mines line the brook's path

It's added joy to be valued
First, is to have a place to serve
A canvass to throw your colours
Some will still prove their crudeness

 If you are running for the accolades
That come from men along the way
You may not run far to get invectives
The purest also from those with you

Mines line up the path to my spring
Need to get them off for my nectar
For this ink not to dry out fast
My pen is not broken.

22 September 2021

This Rain

the rain
the grain
this pain

the rain
the drain
no captain

this rain
blood stain
chained plain

the old rain
the new strain
a rattling refrain

that rain
drops disdain
drains every brain

this unholy rain
will nothing restrain
salvation now a bargain

this riotous rain
upon a villain like Cain
deeply drains the fountain

this rain
wasted brain
and all this pain

my joy my *Ikenga
my peace my *Ọfọ na Ogu

03.02.2022

*Ikenga: among the Igbo people in southeastern Nigeria.
Symbolizes personal strength and achievement.
*Ọfọ na Ogu: Igbo concepts of spiritual justice/ righteousness
and cerebral fairness/uprightness.

Notes: